For Jamie
~ J.S.
For Toby and Charlie
~ T.W.

This edition published for The Book People Ltd,
Hall Wood Avenue, Haydock, St Helens WA11 9UL, by
LITTLE TIGER PRESS
An imprint of Magi Publications
1 The Coda Centre, 189 Munster Road, London SW6 6AW
www.littletigerpress.com
First published in Great Britain 1997
Text © 1997 Julie Sykes
Illustrations © 1997 Tim Warnes
Julie Sykes and Tim Warnes have asserted their rights to
be identified as the author and illustrator of this work under
the Copyright, Designs and Patents Act, 1988.
Printed in Belgium • All rights reserved
ISBN 1 85430 420 8

I don't want to have a bath!

by Julie Sykes

illustrated by Tim Warnes

TED SMART

Little Tiger was very lively.
He liked to play exciting games.
He didn't mean to get dirty,
but somehow he always did.
Then Mummy Tiger would say,
"Little Tiger, you need a bath."
And each time Little Tiger
would answer,
"I don't *want* to have a bath!"

When Mummy Tiger took Little Tiger
down to the river one day to clean
him up, he wouldn't get into the water.
"Bathing is fun," said Mummy Tiger,
but Little Tiger didn't think so.
"I don't want to have a bath!" he cried
and he hurried off into the jungle
before she could make him.

First Little Tiger played with his
good friend, Little Monkey.
They climbed up trees
and swung from vines.
Little Tiger fell off
and dirtied his paws.

Then Mummy Monkey shouted, "Bath time, Little Monkey and Little Tiger, too!"
"I don't want to have a bath!" cried Little Tiger and with a flash of his dirty paws he scurried past Mummy Monkey and into the bushes.

Next Little Tiger went to play with his old friend, Little Bear. They wriggled into bushes and searched for ripe berries. Little Tiger got berry juice all over his face.

Then Daddy Bear growled, "Bath time,
Little Bear and Little Tiger, too!"
"I don't want to have a bath!" said Little Tiger
and twitching his berry stained whiskers he
scampered past Daddy
Bear and down to the
water hole.

Down at the water hole Little Tiger met his dear
friend, Little Elephant. They started to play fight
and Little Elephant squirted mud all over Little
Tiger's coat.

Then Daddy Elephant trumpeted, "Bath time, Little Elephant and Little Tiger, too!"
"I don't want to have a bath!" answered Little Tiger and shaking his muddy paws he raced past Daddy Elephant and out on to the grassy plain.

Little Tiger called on his new friend, Little Rhino next. They charged around in the grass and Little Tiger got grass seeds in his tail. Then Mummy Rhino roared, "Bath time, Little Rhino and Little Tiger, too!"

"I don't want to have a bath!" said Little Tiger and swishing his grassy tail he galloped past Mummy Rhino and back into the jungle.

Little Tiger wondered
who to play with next. The jungle
seemed very quiet and nothing moved,
not even an ant!
Sadly, Little Tiger began to wander home.
But wait – what was that?

Little Tiger looked up
and saw. . .

. . . a handsome peacock, showing
off his tail.

"How beautiful," gasped Little Tiger.
"Will you come and play with me?"

The peacock turned up his beak.
"Play with *you*?" he said. "No thanks!"
"Why not?" asked Little Tiger in surprise.
"Because you're too dirty," said the peacock
scornfully. "You would spoil my lovely feathers.
You need a bath," he added, and tossing his head
off he strutted.

"Stupid peacock!" said
Little Tiger, feeling hurt.
"Of course I don't need
a bath."

Little Tiger wandered on until he reached the river. Playing with his friends had made him thirsty and he stopped to have a drink.

"Who's *that*?" he cried, seeing a reflection in the water. "It can't be me. I'm not *that* dirty."

He leaned over to look more carefully –
and he toppled right in!

Little Tiger spluttered to the surface.
"It *was* me," he cried. "What a mess I looked!"
Quickly Little Tiger began to bath. He splished
and splashed in the warm water. It was fun,
just as Mummy Tiger said it would be.
Once he was clean, Little Tiger climbed back
on to the bank to admire his reflection.
Wouldn't Mummy Tiger be pleased!

Just then, Little Leopard tumbled by. "Hello, Little Tiger," he called. "Will you play with me?" Little Tiger looked at Little Leopard's grubby fur and shook his head. "No thanks," he said. "You're *much* too dirty to play with me. You would spoil my nice clean coat. You need a bath!"

And puffing out his silky chest
Little Tiger hurried home.